To Bill

Betty Jane Wylie

Something Might Happen

Black Moss Press

Published by Black Moss Press, 1939 Alsace Ave.,
Windsor, Ontario, Canada N8W1M5.
Financial assistance towards publication of this book
was provided by the Canada Council
and the Ontario Arts Council.

Black Moss books are distributed by Firefly Books,
Scarborough, Ontario, Canada.

Cover photo: Colin Erricson

Printed and bound in Canada
by Coach House Press, Toronto

ISBN 0-88753-183-0

Acknowledgements
Special thanks to Don Coles, Richard Teleky, and Rod Willmot,
for their advice, assistance and encouragement.

Suddenly your eyes are marbles
    and mine are jellies.

Your throat has closed
    and mine can't open.

Look at me, look at me.

I don't want to look in your mirror,
  you might still be there.

Someone put your glasses on the dresser.

Both of us unseeing.

Your watch stopped
  twelve hours after you did
  quietly ticking on your wrist.

Self-winding,
  it got your message

  and unwound

Where did all these people come from?

Like a treed animal
I wait for them to leave.

Huddle

  drink coffee and whisper
  try to understand
  a life has stopped.

I can't think what I'm
  doing here in the dark.

I can't think what I'm doing.

I can't think.

The Pucci tie was new last week
    you look so handsome in the dark blue suit
    it has a scarlet lining
    the glasses are for the children's sake

perhaps they won't notice the closed eyes

'How kind of you to let me come'
'How good it is to see you'
'Say hello to mother'
'Don't let me delay you'

Flit bravely from flower to flower

You aren't here

My father looked like a Mississippi gambler
    mouth as thin as a string tie.
But he took a while to die
    so they had to work on him.

But you
    you look

I never saw you this way before.

The gold at your wrists,
  masks of Comedy and Tragedy,
  are in there with you.

My last gift
  they arrived late
  but you insisted they go under the tree,
  your last.

Old kings buried with their weapons
jewels idols
cups of gold.

Range 16, lot 43 –
you have a different address now

Where we used to live
I merely reside

Was yesterday real?
Were you?

How can I be angry?

You never left a party
    before it was time
    always helped me clean up

Always leave them laughing
    quit while you're ahead
    exit while they want you

We had our pictures taken for new passports
    just weeks ago.

Your face is smiling, confident

No one looks good in a passport picture
    you did

I am still earth-bound

No visa

I have to say all your farewells for you
    and then

I have to say all mine

There is an afterglow
    even now

I have sunspots

I hope they're you

Yesterday we assumed
    all the time in the world.

Each other's audience
    played for pleasure
    closed, private

Now I am brass
    my laughter is dust

I have all the time in the world.

This is your house
    and nothing works

    the heating system has stopped
    the blinds stick
    the windows are broken

it is determined to stop functioning

Will someone please turn on a light?

I am water
I slip across peoples' faces and minds
    leaving no mark

    opaque inert
No shores
    no source
    no colour
    shape, flow

One night the phone rings

Is it you?

I know where you are
    no need to call
    your line is no longer in service
    mine doesn't reach

    the phone persists and the illusion

    you are on the other end
    as close as my telephone

I would go mad of course

You talked to the sparrows
    huddling at our bird feeder.
    'Tell your friends,' you'd say,
    'Everyone is welcome.'

You flirted with the cat
    cradling him in your arms
    telling him his dignity
    wasn't worth being lonely.

You rough-housed the dog
    rendering him vulnerable
    with a well-placed finger
    just behind his ear.

You cherished the children
    pursuing them with laughter
    hoarding their differences
    a treasure of absurdities.

You talked to me
    flirted
    cradled
    rough-housed
    cherished
    treasured.

Could you have stood this pain?

Like a stain that spreads and colours
  like ink in a blotter

Most of the time I'm invisible.

They say you're most alive
    when you fear for your life.
I don't fear for mine
    but I could wish I were less alive.

I never asked to be a heroine.

I had some vague vision:
    the two of us
    facing the sunset together
    earnestly puttering around the kitchen
    walking religiously
    wearing scarves drinking Ovaltine.

Or else the two of us
    overturning once and fatally on a four-lane highway

    exploding in a jet plane

You spoiled the scenarios.

I have no script now
    no script and no fear.

I always got along very well without you, I
    function smoothly
    keeping appointments fulfilling
    obligations taking time to
    read, remembering my vitamins and my
    careful driving

You were probably hazardous to my health
    certainly addictive

You turned me upside inside
    bubbles of oxygen in my blood, heart pumping
    adrenalin through my entire system

Already the withdrawal symptoms are alarming

I will get along very well without you

    cool

If I lie on this earth long enough
    will I feel you stirring beneath me?

If I lie here long enough
    could I put down roots?

Tired of waiting?

I am.

The stone is new every visit
    time doesn't soften it nor
    apologetic geraniums woeful yews

I wither too

Come home with me

This is no place for either of us.

The entrance is simple enough
    crosses on the white walls, polished

Every Sunday prim and scarlet in my choir gown, singing
    I follow your coffin down the centre aisle

Room upon room empty white silent, searing
    no stairs up out down

Every Sunday a white box

I am building a wall, carefully,
 choosing placing each brick
 a free-standing wall, no support

One side to be plastered, carefully
 with a smooth facade, painted too –
 three coats

Finished, I will go behind my wall
 hunker down, scratch a hole
 for my bones

Your head was my home for so long I
  walked naked, beautiful
  innocence hanging on a hook

  there

  here is where I laid our babies

  not out here

My blood remains in my body
  uncut
I will not let it.

My eyes remain in my head
  unshut
  I will not set them.

If I'm ever going to find you again
  I'll need all my faculties
  and I know no short cuts
      of knife razor distance time

My skin is cold.

You slip in and out of my present

Or am I slipping in and out of your past?

Soon your clothes will be out of style

Soon you will be younger than I

At first when you left
    there was a white space like a blank

Then the white space moved inside
    no bigger than a moth, testing
    wings against walls

It has taken longer to grow you than a child

Never to be delivered

I bleed
    eggs babies dreams unrequited love

How dare I?

My blood negotiates a separate peace

My blood has no right to flow or sing

I did not agree to this

We were in this same water together last year
  naked in the water with you
  touching the white undersides of my breasts

Your body does not bear thinking about
  but I think about it

Your mouth is full of clay
  and mine still longs for yours

You are weightless
  and I am uncovered

This bed is the funeral pyre
    his body the fuel
    I the sacrifice

Wrong.

            He is.

He turns to my light and heat
    finding the live coal at my dead centre

He is a god of light leaping dancing flying up

He crumbles like a cardboard carton
    shuddering collapsing

The light fades

I am singed blackened and still here

He makes me lose my present, my balance

Not tender –
    brash horny self-assured

He takes my mouth
    and makes me lose my mind

Your love is no longer a perfect circle
    about my finger or heart.

I have strung you on a chain
    about my throat.
My finger is free to love again.
My throat is not.

The chain burns marks the pulse
    rising gleaming
    with the beat of the unencircled heart.

Too light to throttle

The strength of the chain is time.

Throats melt
    fingers wither
    chains rattle
    hearts falter.

Do you remember the birch trees?

You turned, kissed me, hands rustling like leaves
    stripping away white layers of me.

Sighing trembling with them I stretched, arched but
    did not fall
    to the explicit ground.

I wish I had.

I am sticky with sex
    gummed up to my eyeballs.

My eyes are flypapers
    and I catch men's eyes like flies.

They catch and hold and stick
    swinging on my flypaper eyes.

Unstick me who can.

I am oozing with sex
    dropping clots of it as I sashay by.

A quicksand catching men's feet
    sucking them into my depths.

Ten men and a horse
    gone without a trace.
Never know it to look at my face.

I never resisted him.

He moved into me, passive,
    as if invited, making himself at home.
I gave him your place, pipe, favourite things.

If he was surprised, he didn't say so.

Occasionally I fought, ripping clothes,
    slashing with my teeth, hurling myself at him
    as if he were a wall I had to tear down.

He is a life-size demonstrator kit, Erector set,
He has a limited range

I play with all his moving parts, reconstructing you

Maybe he's used to being a sample

New model, better condition,
    too slick too glossy no bumps hollows dents scars

His face isn't familiar

I recognize his mouth
    shaping mine tasting different.

His hands are bold fingers dropping
    bits and pieces of other women all over me.

I become a piece of patchwork, quilt
    feather-stitched to cover his bed.

Once in my own bed I was a blanket for my true love,
    electric.

I have no controls now

Seeking warmth I generate no heat.

Has he ever laid a ghost before?

He licks my salt.

I have been lured by the assertion of his flesh
and mine.

Shall I thank him or scream?

When I open my eyes I am surprised

He changes my focus

Looking beyond him I see your image
    blurring, dimming as it falls

He comforts me for not being dead

Who ever would have thought that
  I, I. I!!!
  would warm my hands at another heart?

He is young over his head, floundering

At first Sir Lancelot
    helping a lady in distress

Suddenly sincere, a social worker seeking
    servicing me with selfish mouth and young arms

Now I have cost him something
    he is not so sure.

My speech overwhelms, body drowns

Poor Boy Scout
Stay away from widows.

Your absence
    continues to surprise me.

How long is this going to go on?

Halfway
    between then and now
Somewhere
    between now and there
I walk
    frequently without pain
    capable of laughter.

The tunnel is shorter than it was.

Light at the end
    no longer flickers and recedes.

I begin to notice the walls
    interesting lichens and mosses
    no two alike.

I am present,
    tense but present.

I continue.

Something might happen
    sun might shine

    seed might burst.